Sasha loves to do what
everyone in San Francisco
loves to do . . .
Eat.
See the sights.
Then eat some more!

Sasha the San Francisco Sea Lion
Copyright © 2003
Ron Berman and Frank Hill
www.sashasealion.com

This book is distributed by:
Smith Novelty Co., San Francisco, California
888.861.7626
www.smithnovelty.com

United States Copyright Office #TXu 550 246 • 12/28/92

Printed in Korea

Sasha
THE SAN FRANCISCO
Sea Lion

By Ron Berman
Illustrations Frank Hill

Sasha the Sea Lion, a friend of mine,
lived in the sea off Pier 39
on San Francisco's beautiful bay,
a perfect place for sea lions to play.

Folks came from near and from Cleveland too,
to see the things a sea lion can do;
like waddling and wading and just having fun,
then going to sleep in the warm noonday sun.

One day Sasha was enjoying a nap,
when he awoke to find a map in his lap.
It showed all the places people can go,
in the magical city called San Francisco.

"If they can go there, why can't I?"
said Sasha with a wishful sigh.
"There's so much to do and so much to see,
San Francisco is calling me."

So now his adventure was about to begin,
as he hailed a taxi and jumped right in.

First he went to the Fairmont Hotel,
on a hill where famous buildings dwell.
He was met by a bellman wearing a grin,
who graciously checked the sea lion in.

When he got to his room,
he barked for room service
and made the people next door,
a bride and groom, nervous.

Soon a waiter named Jake
showed up with a steak,
which Sasha the Sea Lion
did not want to take.
For his one hungry wish
was not a meat dish
but a beautiful,
bountiful kettle of fish.

The hotel guests enjoyed the sight
of Sasha sashaying out daytime and night.
The grown-ups would giggle and the kids would shriek,
as they followed our Sasha through a wonderful week.

Monday

He went to Coit Tower,
the view was a treat, then
skedaddled down Lombard,
the crookedest street.
He entered North Beach and
proceeded to buy a mackerel
and halibut hot pizza pie!

He dressed in a coat all cuddly and warm
for Monday night baseball where the Giants perform.
He squealed and applauded (sea lions don't shout),
when the hometown pitcher struck ten batters out
as he munched on a hot dog but much preferred trout.

Tuesday

He went to the Museum of Modern Art
where he saw a painting that gave him a start.
It was one that made the critics applaud,
but was actually painted by his young brother Claude.

That night he looked like a million bucks,
all dressed up in a rented tux.
At Davies Hall where the orchestras play
but the trumpeter was absent, a traffic delay.

He jumped on the stage to save the day,
with a solo from "Carmen" composed by Bizet.
(It's a fact I really don't have to tell,
but horns are one thing sea lions play well.)

Wednesday

He went to the ocean, jumped right in
and took a swim to marvelous Marin.
He cavorted with cousins named Bertram and Midge
and saluted commuters on the Golden Gate Bridge.

He swam back to the wharf
and took in some Jazz,
then boarded a ferry to Alcatraz.

It's the island prison
where the curious crave,
to see where they kept
folks who didn't behave.

He saw every cell in every cell block
and proclaimed the island "The Jailhouse Rock."

Thursday

He rented a bike and just for a lark
went for a ride in Golden Gate Park.
He honked at the birds and sniffed at
the breeze and waved to the squirrels as
they ran up the trees. Then he stopped
for his favorite picnic spread of
sardines and jelly on sourdough bread.

Friday

He was touring Chinatown when it started to rain,
found a cozy cafe and ordered Chow Mein
with sea weed and urchins and noodles and kippers,
though chop sticks are hard to handle with flippers.

He went back outside where
his evening was made,
when he rode on the dragon
in the New Year's Parade.
At the sight of Sasha the crowd
gave a squeal, you'd think it was
"The Year of the Seal."

Saturday

He arrived at the Cliff House to be with the flocks
of tourists in their fanciest frocks
and waved to his cousins who lived on the rocks
while he munched on a breakfast of bagels and lox.

Down on the beach he played in the sand,
jumped in the ocean as it lapped on the land,
rode on a surfboard and soon was viewed,
as a real cool sea lion surfer dude.

Sunday

He slept until noon then
checked out at two to hob nob
Nob Hill and admire the view.
He was waddling about and
doing quite well, when
he suddenly heard the
sound of a bell.

Along the tracks that climbed up the hill
he saw a sight that gave him a thrill.
"It's the cable car," said a little old man.
So right to the cable car our sea lion ran.
The bell-ringer clanged and the passengers roared,
as Sasha the Sea Lion clambered aboard.

Now I know it's silly and foolish by golly,
for the bravest sea lion to ride on a trolley.
But oh, he had a spectacular time
from the start of the ride to the end of the line
where he waddled back to Pier 39.

He was greeted by applause and sea lion chants
from his brothers and sisters and uncles and aunts.

And even though there's no place like home,
Sasha the Sea Lion still wanted to roam.
He had heard that New York was a traveler's delight
and he planned to fly there when the prices were right.